Olaudah Equiano
From Slavery to Freedom

Written by Paul Thomas

Illustrated by Victor Ambrus

Contents

Collins

Olaudah Equiano

This is the story of a man who became a slave as a child but eventually helped to put an end to slavery. His name was Olaudah Equiano.

This portrait of Olaudah Equiano is from his **autobiography**.

Slavery

Slavery is when the law allows one person to own another, like a piece of property. Slave owners can make that person do whatever they want. Slaves have no **human rights.** They work under very harsh conditions and can be bought and sold.

The history of slavery goes back thousands of years. It was a part of life in Ancient Egypt, Ancient Greece and the Roman **Empire**.

Later, in the 15th and 16th centuries, British, Dutch, French, Portuguese and Spanish traders explored the coast of Africa looking for people to sell as slaves. These people were then shipped to the **colonies** of America and the **Caribbean** to work as slave **labour**. It is estimated that up to 20 million people were taken as slaves from Africa to the Americas through the Middle Passage.

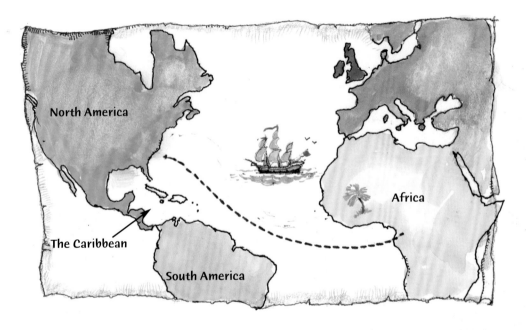

The Middle Passage was the journey that the slave ships took from West Africa across the Atlantic Ocean to America. The ships were packed full of slaves. Many of them died of disease and **malnutrition** before they reached land.

Olaudah's early life

Olaudah Equiano was born around the year 1745 in the part of Africa that is now called Nigeria. He was the youngest son of a village **elder**. His family expected him to follow in his father's footsteps and become a chief.

However when Olaudah was only 11 years old, he and his sister were kidnapped from their village by **slavers.** The slavers ignored their cries for mercy. As Olaudah wrote in his autobiography many years later, "the only comfort we had was in being in one another's arms all that night, and bathing each other with our tears."

The next day Olaudah was separated from his sister. He never saw her again. He was forced into a slave boat and chained to other prisoners. The boat sailed all the way across the Atlantic Ocean to North America. This must have been a lonely and terrifying journey.

In the days of slavery, children bought and sold as slaves had
to do whatever their owners told them to. Olaudah was bought
by a British Royal Navy officer called Michael Pascal, who took
him to sea. When the ships were in dock, Olaudah stayed with
friends of Pascal, who encouraged him to go to school. He was
very excited about this and soon learnt to read and write.
However, when the ships sailed again Olaudah had to leave
school and go back to sea.

War at sea

At this time, Britain and France were at war. Both countries wanted control of North America and the Caribbean. During the many battles at sea, Olaudah had the very dangerous job of carrying gunpowder to each of the ship's guns. Even though he was forced to work, he worked hard and was very brave and loyal.

During wartime, the crew of a ship shared the value of the treasure they stole from other ships. Olaudah hoped that he would be given a share of this, but his greatest dream was of being given his freedom.

However, Olaudah never got his prize money as Pascal sold him to another sea captain. Olaudah tried to resist, but was threatened with having his throat cut. He was taken to the island of Montserrat in the Caribbean where he was sold again to a merchant called Robert King, who owned a sugar cane **plantation**. His dream of being free had been destroyed.

Plantation life

Although Olaudah didn't work on the plantation, he soon became familiar with the horrors of the plantation world. He saw slave owners living in luxury while their slaves lived in tiny, cramped cabins that weren't fit for human beings. He saw slaves working in terrible conditions, starved and beaten by their owners.

Slaves were punished for not working fast enough, being late, speaking back to their masters, or trying to run away. A slave could even be punished for being weak or too ill to work. The punishments would include imprisonment, torture and whippings. The ultimate punishment was death – on the plantations the killing of a slave was never regarded as murder.

Olaudah realised that only his education had saved him from being sent to work on the plantation. He was considered a valuable slave because he could read, write and work with numbers. He was given the job of "gauger", someone who weighed and measured the sugar cane. But every day Olaudah saw the cruelty of slavery. This made him determined to be free himself and to fight for the freedom of all slaves.

Although Olaudah was a slave, he was paid for his work as a gauger. He saved every penny he earned, eating very little and working very hard. After three long years, he had saved £40. In today's money, that would be equal to £2,000. This was the price of his freedom. Robert King accepted the £40 and let him go free.

Freedom!

It had taken Olaudah ten hard years, but at the age of 21 he was able to go to England as a free man. He wrote, "My feet scarcely touched the ground, for they were winged with joy...this was the happiest day I had ever experienced."

Soon after, Olaudah arrived in England. He trained as a hairdresser, then later went back to sea as a **steward** on board a ship. In 1768 he worked for Doctor Charles Irving, who allowed him to continue his education. Over the next few years, Olaudah went on different voyages to the **Mediterranean** and the Caribbean.

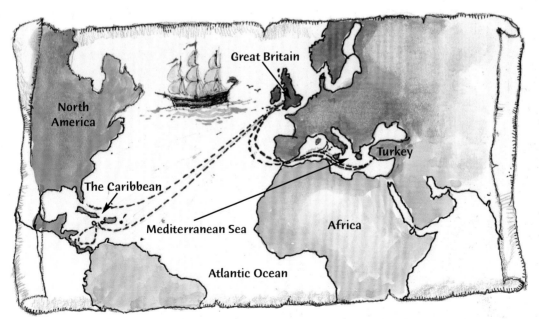

Great Britain

North America

Turkey

The Caribbean

Mediterranean Sea

Africa

Atlantic Ocean

Exploration

In 1773 Olaudah took on a new challenge. He joined an important **expedition** with **explorers** who hoped to find a new route to Asia across the North Pole. This undiscovered route was known as the Northwest Passage. The expedition set off on a ship called *The Racehorse* and took four months. Olaudah saw many unusual sights such as giant icebergs and polar bears.

Passage Through the Ice, June 16, 1818 by Sir John Ross

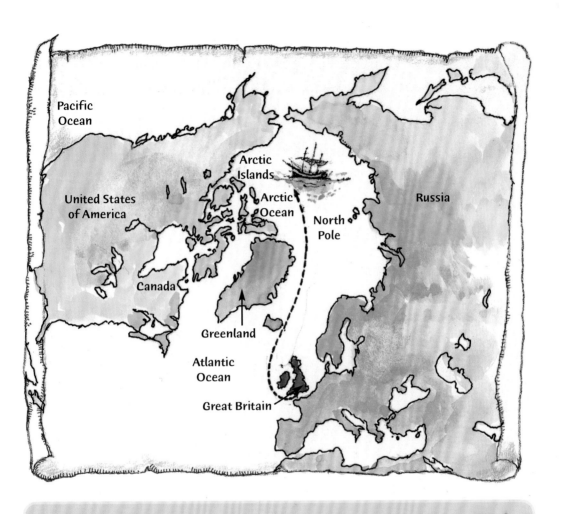

From the 15th century to the 20th century explorers tried to discover a route from the Atlantic Ocean to the Pacific Ocean around the Arctic islands of Canada. Explorers hoped that a route could be found that would provide a shorter journey for ships from Europe to Asia. The route, named the Northwest Passage, was finally discovered in 1906, but as the **Arctic Ocean** freezes for most of the year regular voyages weren't possible.

However, when *The Racehorse* reached the Arctic Ocean, disaster struck. The temperature fell and the sea froze, so that Olaudah's ship was trapped in a sea of ice. The crew was terrified. The ice could easily squeeze *The Racehorse* to pieces. The captain ordered everyone to cut the ice from around the ship to stop the ship breaking up. Olaudah worked hard with the other sailors. The thought of dying in the icy waters of the Arctic filled him and the rest of the crew with terror.

After 11 days, the weather became warmer and the ice around the ship began to melt. The crew was now able to sail into open water, glad to have escaped a frozen death. The ship managed to **set a course** for home and eventually arrived in London a month later. Although the Northwest Passage hadn't been found this time, the expedition in *The Racehorse* was still regarded as a great scientific success.

A new plantation

After this adventure Olaudah joined a group of people who tried to set up a new type of plantation on the Caribbean coast of **Central America.** They wanted to establish a kinder plantation that would provide the slaves with better food, housing and medical care. This was in 1775, a time when slavery was still a normal part of society. Perhaps even Olaudah didn't yet dare to dream that slavery could be **abolished** completely.

The Caribbean

Central America

The group included Englishmen like Dr Irving, who knew that Olaudah had already worked on plantations and hoped he would reassure the slaves that they would be treated fairly. Also in the group were Miskito Indians, who were returning to their home after living in England for 12 months. They also hoped to set up a new kind of plantation.

20

Olaudah set sail for the Caribbean. But when the ship docked in Central America he was cheated of his wages by the captain of his ship. Olaudah also nearly became a slave again when the captain refused to believe that he had bought his freedom.

With the help of the Indians Olaudah managed to escape to Jamaica in a homemade canoe. There he found Dr Irving, who tried to help him get back the money he was owed. They went to several magistrates in Jamaica to get justice, but none would believe Olaudah's word against the captain's.

Escape!

Olaudah heard that the captain was sailing to Jamaica and had threatened to kill Olaudah for calling him a thief. Olaudah feared for his life. So he decided to leave Jamaica quickly and, with Dr Irving's help, gained a place on board a ship to England.

He arrived in Plymouth in January 1777, grateful to the doctor for saving him. However, a few months later Olaudah heard that Dr Irving had died in Jamaica from eating poisoned fish. He was sorry to have lost such a good and loyal friend.

A new adventure

Olaudah realised that attitudes towards black people needed to change and he gave up the idea of having a **humane** plantation for slaves. After seven years working as a steward, mainly on ships to North America, he became involved with the anti-slavery movement in London.

The Society for the Abolition of the Slave Trade was founded in Britain in 1787. It was started by Granville Sharp and Thomas Clarkson. Most members of the society were Quakers, a religious group that believed in equality for everyone. Another important campaigner was William Wilberforce, a Member of Parliament.

Granville Sharp

Olaudah met many important anti-slavery **campaigners** like
Granville Sharp, who invited him to become part of the Sierra
Leone **resettlement** project. The aim of this project was to change
the lives of the poor Africans who lived on the streets in
London by taking them to the African country of Sierra Leone.
They planned to set up a colony where there would be justice
and equality for all and where slavery would be outlawed.

The Africans had been brought to England against their will
so the **abolitionists** assumed that they would want to return.
Enough people were persuaded to take part in the voyage with
promises of a better life in Africa, although some didn't even know
where they were going until they were on board the ship.

Olaudah remembered his own experiences when he had
attempted to set up a new plantation in the Caribbean and hoped
that this new plan would work. Granville Sharp promised him
that this time things would be different. Olaudah trusted Sharp,
so he joined the project.

Olaudah's job was to make sure that enough food and equipment
were bought for the voyage and to establish the new colony
in Sierra Leone. It was a very important job.

Corruption

Olaudah soon found out that **corrupt** officials around him were keeping some of the money and not buying enough food and equipment. When he told people about this corruption, only his close friends believed him.

The corrupt officials had too many powerful friends and saw to it that Olaudah lost his job. Granville Sharp tried to fight against this, but he was ignored.

Eventually Olaudah was proved right about the Sierra Leone colony. The lack of food made it difficult for the Africans to survive the long voyage. Those who completed the journey soon found that they didn't have the equipment to grow crops. Of the 374 people who made the original voyage, only 60 survived the first four years.

Although Olaudah was very disappointed with the outcome of the Sierra Leone project, he continued to work for the anti-slavery movement. The movement was growing and Olaudah had become a strong abolitionist. He was also inspired by the **revolution** in France in 1789 and the slave uprising on the Caribbean island of Haiti two years later.

In 1791 slaves, for the first time, had **risen up** in protest against their conditions and treatment on the Caribbean island of St Dominque (now called Haiti). Under the brilliant leadership of Toussaint L'Ouverture, the slaves defeated the foreign rulers of the island and declared their freedom in 1801. Although L'Ouverture was killed in 1803, Haiti became the first **independent** black country in the Caribbean.

Toussaint L'Ouverture

Becoming an author

Olaudah then decided to do something that very few black people had done before. He wrote a book about his life as a slave and as a free man. He hoped that by writing his autobiography he would achieve two aims. The first would be to describe the tragedy of the slave trade and to gain support for the anti-slavery movement. The second would be to show by his actions that black and white people were equal and that they should have equal rights.

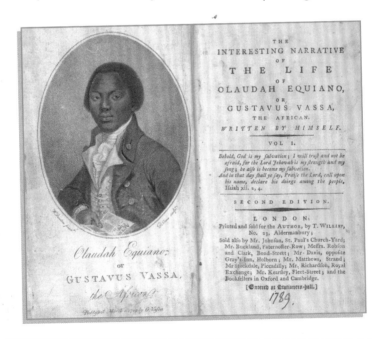

It was common practice for owners to give slaves new names. Olaudah had been given the name Gustavus Vassa.

Olaudah's book was a great success throughout Great Britain and America and was **translated** into Dutch, German and Russian. Many famous and important people read and admired the book.

Olaudah became a popular public speaker. He toured the whole of Great Britain, reading from his book and promoting the abolition of slavery. Money from both the sale of the book and from his readings transformed his life and allowed Olaudah for the first time to live a genuinely independent life.

A new family

In 1792 Olaudah fell in love with an Englishwoman named
Susanna Cullen. They married and settled down together
in Cambridgeshire, England. They had two daughters, Anna Maria
in 1793 and Joanna in 1795. This was a very happy time for them.

However, not long after Joanna was born, tragedy struck Olaudah and his family when Susanna died.

In 1797, when he was about 52, Olaudah himself died. Four months after Olaudah's death, his daughter Anna Maria died. Joanna was the only survivor of the family.

We know very little about what happened to Joanna, except that on her 21st birthday, she inherited £950 from her father's will, worth about £100,000 today.

Remembering Olaudah

Olaudah had been forced into slavery as a child, but he went on to achieve a great deal in his life and died a rich and famous man. He died knowing that his work and ideas had played a big part in changing people's attitudes towards slavery.

The slave trade was abolished in the UK by an **Act of Parliament** in 1807. British captains who were caught trading in slaves were fined £100 for every slave found on board. However, this didn't stop some captains. When boats were checked for slaves, the captains would throw their slaves overboard to avoid being fined. Eventually, in 1833, a new law was passed which gave every slave in the **British Empire** their freedom.

In the United States of America, though, slavery was still legal. There were several groups that were against slavery, but in most of the country it was allowed.

However, in 1861 the northern part of the USA fought against the southern part in the American **Civil War**. One of the reasons for the war was that the northern states didn't want slavery to be allowed to increase, but the southern states were very keen for slavery to expand.

After four years and thousands of deaths the northern states won the Civil War. Slavery was then abolished in the United States of America.

Olaudah didn't live to see the day when slavery was abolished, but he is remembered for all that he did to end its horrors.

a plaque put up in October 2000 on the house where Olaudah lived in London

CITY OF WESTMINSTER

OLAUDAH
EQUIANO
(1745 – 1797)
"THE AFRICAN"

LIVED AND PUBLISHED HERE
IN 1789 HIS AUTOBIOGRAPHY
ON SUFFERING THE
BARBARITY OF SLAVERY,
WHICH PAVED THE WAY
FOR ITS ABOLITION

Glossary

abolished	when a law or custom is ended
abolitionists	people who campaign for a law to be abolished
Act of Parliament	a law brought into force by the government of the country
Arctic Ocean	the ocean between the North Pole and the northern edges of North America, Europe and Asia
autobiography	the story of a person's life written by themself
British Empire	a large group of countries that used to be ruled by Great Britain
campaigners	people who take part in supporting a cause they feel strongly about

Caribbean	the chain of islands from Florida to the north coast of South America
Central America	the region from the southern border of Mexico to the northern border of Colombia
civil war	a war fought between people of the same country
colonies	areas of land that the people of another country settle in and control
corrupt	people who are dishonest and can be persuaded to commit crimes
elder	an important and older member of a family, tribe or community
empire	a group of countries ruled by one country

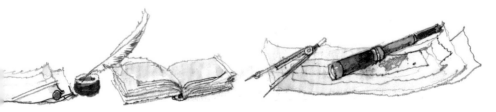

expedition	an organised journey made in order to find something in a remote place
explorers	people who travel to a distant place in order to learn about it
humane	kind-hearted and merciful
human rights	the right of everyone to live and speak freely
independent	not depending on any person or thing for help, money or support
labour	to work hard
malnutrition	bad health because of not having enough food to eat
Mediterranean	the largest inland sea in the world, between Europe, Africa and Asia

plantation	a large area of land where crops such as cotton, tobacco, sugar or tea are planted
resettlement	the transportation of people to a new place
revolution	the removal of a government by force and violence
risen up	rebelled
set a course	sail towards
slavers	men who kidnapped people to sell into slavery
steward	a man whose job is to look after the passengers on a ship or aircraft
translated	put into another language

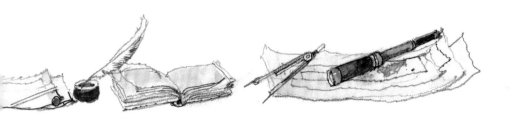

Index

A timeline

Year	Event

1745 Olaudah Equiano is born in what is now Nigeria.

1756 He and his sister are kidnapped by slavers.

1766 Olaudah earns enough money to buy his own freedom.

1773 Olaudah joins an expedition to find the Northwest Passage.

1775 Olaudah travels to Central America to set up a new type of plantation.

1786 Olaudah becomes part of the Sierra Leone resettlement project.

1787 The Society for the Abolition of the Slave Trade is founded in Britain.

1789 ↓	The French Revolution begins. Its ideas of liberty for all encourages rebellion in the slave colonies.
1789 ↓	Olaudah publishes his autobiography. It becomes a bestseller.
1792 ↓	Olaudah marries Susanna Cullen.
1797 ↓	Olaudah dies.
1807 ↓	The British Parliament passes the law for the abolition of the slave trade across the Atlantic Ocean.
1833 ↓	Slavery is abolished in the British colonies.
1865	Slavery is abolished in the United States at the end of the American Civil War.

Ideas for guided reading

Learning objectives: identify the features of recounted texts including introduction to orientate reader, chronological sequence, supporting illustrations, use of connectives, degree of formality; discuss the purpose of note taking and how this influences nature of notes made; write recounts based on subject or personal experience for a close friend; tell a story using notes

Curriculum links: Citizenship: Developing good relationships and respecting differences between people; Realise the nature and consequences of racism

Interest words: abolitionists, campaigners, elder, human rights, malnutrition, plantation, Quakers, resettlement

Resources: a globe

Getting started

This book can be read over two or more guided reading sessions.

- Explain to children that you are going to research the life of Olaudah Equiano. Read the blurb and encourage prediction.

- Ask one of the children to read aloud pp2–5.

- Read the map on p5 and trace with a finger the middle passage onto a globe.

- Discuss what kind of text this is and the purpose of the pages read (*to orientate the reader to idea and history of slavery*).

- Discuss the purpose of the following chapters – to tell the life of Olaudah and describe what it was like to be a slave.

- Ask the children the features they would expect to find in a recount (*past tense, time connectives, chronological sequence*) and scan to find examples.

Reading and responding

- Ask the children to read through silently and be prepared to discuss: *What made Olaudah an exceptional man?*

- Discuss what made Olaudah exceptional and encourage children to justify their opinion with reference to the text and facts.